THE DINOSAUR WHO DISCOVERED HAMBURGERS

Scout loved being a dinosaur. Of course, being a dinosaur had its perks.

Dinosaurs were able to run faster...

...roar louder...

...and were stronger than all the other animals.

But the best part of being a dinosaur was that they were all big foodies! They loved going out to restaurants and enjoyed eating different foods!

There were lots of dishes to choose from. Sushi, Chicken Nuggets, Pizza and more...but Scout always felt like there was a great dish that was still missing.

Scout decided to go seek it out...
and so began the journey.

Scout packed binoculars, a magnifying glass, a plate, a knife, a spoon, a fork and a map.

Scout searched far and wide, venturing through treacherous terrain.

Scout climbed the highest mountains...

...and waded through the thickest swamps.

Scout was exhausted and ready to give up. Just as Scout was about to turn back, a strange forest appeared into view.

It seemed the forest had oddly shaped fruit. Scout used the binoculars to look closer.

OF COURSE!

This was a Bread Forest! It was filled with bread buns as far as the eye could see...toasted buns, sesame buns and brioche buns! Scout grabbed some and continued on.

Scout left the forest and entered a valley filled with beautiful flowers.

But again, something was odd about these flowers...Scout took out the magnifying glass and took a closer look.

It looked like the petals of these flowers were made of pickles!

OF COURSE!

These were Pickle Flowers!

Scout grabbed some and continued on.

Scout kept walking and came across two strange rivers. One river was red and the other was yellow. Scout got close to the rivers and took out the spoon.

Scout dipped the spoon into each river and had a taste...one was sweet and one was sour!

OF COURSE!

These were the great rivers of Ket-Chup and Mus-Tard! Overjoyed, Scout packed some of each.

Scout continued on and wandered by some large bushes that had a wonderful aroma.

Scout reached into the backpack, pulled out the fork and knife, and started to poke into the bushes. Out came a meat patty and slice of bacon grilled to perfection!

OF COURSE!

These were Bacon and Patty Bushes!

Scout now had lots of ingredients and flavors to work with and started to head home, passing back through the rivers of Ket-Chup and Mus-Tard, walking again through the fields of Pickle Flowers, trekking once more through the Bread Forest...

..wading back through the thickest swamps...

...re-crossing the hottest deserts...

...and climbing back down the highest mountains.

Scout, finally at home, went into the kitchen
and began to plan the meal.

Scout tried many different combinations, but none of them seemed right.

Then it came to Scout...

OF COURSE!

Bun →

Ketchup →

Pickles →

Bacon →

Patty →

Mustard →

and Bun! →

The perfect order for the perfect dish! Now to taste our creation!

Scout took a bite. It was good, but it still felt like something was missing. So Scout decided to visit Dr. Ham, the smartest dinosaur scientist in town, to see what they could come up with together.

Dr. Ham showed Scout the newest
technology in food processing.

Scout stood and watched Dr. Ham's team toil and tinker with their formulas to come up with just the right addition to the dish.

The machines hummed, the beakers boiled and the gauges whirred. Voila! After the smoke cleared, all the dinosaurs looked upon their creation with wonder.

With the new creations ready for tasting,
Dr. Ham began official scientific tests.

Scout thought the names were a little long, and suggested they name them tomato, onion and lettuce instead.

The other dinosaurs agreed and were amazed at Scout's genius.

Scout took slices of the new foods and added them into the dish.

OF COURSE!

This is what was missing. Scout tasted the creation and knew this was the perfect dish!

Mmm...

Scout shared this discovery with the other dinosaurs, who all agreed that they loved this dish. Scout, thankful for all of Dr. Ham's help, decided to name the dish after the doctor.

What is your full name Dr. Ham?

My full name is Dr. Ham Burger the 12th. I come from a long line of Burgers.

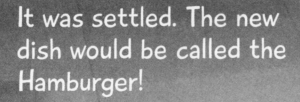

It was settled. The new dish would be called the Hamburger!

All the dinosaurs loved eating Scout's new dish...

...even the Velociraptor Food Guide gave it 6 claws way up!

News of the dish spread quickly
and everyone had to try it.
IT WAS A HIT!

The dish was so popular that the dinosaurs even made an International Hamburger Day!

Even movies were made to show how this amazing new dish was discovered!

Scout felt happy and complete.
The perfect dish was found and all was
right in the world.

THE END

Check out our other great books!

Available on Amazon